Sleep overs

After four long years in college, Autumn and I finally graduated from college. I got a degree in Architecture, and she got a degree in engineering. We both have jobs already lined up thanks to her mom Summer and dad Thad.

Summer and Thad were very proud of us graduating. They shed tears at the graduation ceremony. Thad got us both white Audi A4's and a new apartments 5 miles from Miami beach. Autumn and I both attended the University of Miami aka the U.

Summer, Autumn and Thad helped us move into our new luxury apartments. We were finally able to live on our own with the help of Summer and Thad. Six months later, I was assigned to a project designing a new stadium. I was put in charge of seat detail for the whole stadium including luxury boxes and press boxes.

I wasn't given a budget, but I knew they probably didn't want to spend the whole budget on it. I got samples for low end seats, medium seats and high-end seats for the luxury boxes. It took hours to render all the seats into the stadium. When it was complete the bosses were very happy with the final product.

After work, I went home to relax and eat something before I went to my workout. I came back to take a shower then relax. The weekend came and Summer asked me if she could visit. I said sure and invited her over. When the bell rang, I answered it and wow. She wore a short ass summer dress with her suitcase.

Summer and Thad live 15 minutes away but yet Summer had a suitcase. I invited her inside and she put her stuff away in the guest bedroom. We sat on the couch and talked about my job and whatever Summer was up too at the moment.

Damn Summer's sweet white thighs were killing me. I said I miss you Summer and she said I missed you too, especially all the hugs, even the boner hugs in the mornings. I said sorry about that Summer, she said its ok I didn't mind your big hard cock glued to my big ass. I said you do have an amazing ass. Summer giggled, I said how come you didn't do or say anything about that until now.

Summer said I wanted to encourage you, but I couldn't. Thad and Autumn were home, your hard dick made me wet every time you hugged me from behind. I said really, I'm glad I made your pussy wet. Summer said do you have any dishes that need washing. I said I do have some dishes that need washing.

Summer smiled at me and winked at me. She got up and jiggled to the kitchen. I got up and watched her at the sink. I went for it and hugged her from behind. Summer moaned out loud and said this brings back such wonderful memories. I kissed her neck as I put my hands around her waist. I grind my hard cock into her big ass. She grinds right back at me that's when I reached up and grabbed her big ass titties.

I moaned oh Summer, I want you so bad. She said I want you too honey, fuck me. I dropped my pants and reached around to massage Summer's pussy. I felt nothing but her wet pussy, I thought she came to my apartment with no panties on, wow.

I bent her over and shoved my black cock up her tight cunt forcefully. Summer moaned oh god your finally deep in my white pussy, fuck me hard baby. I held her hips and started fucking Summer hard. It drove her wild as she took all of me. I felt her pussy vibrate and the accompanying cream on my shaft.

Summer said oh yeah, my black stud, I came all over your big wonderful dick. I showed her pussy no mercy ramming the shit out of her cunt. I reached the point of no return and I filled Summer with my warm seed.

I moaned oh god as I gave her my last squirts of cream. Summer said oh wow that was intense and worth the wait. She turned around and kissed me like we have never kissed before, I grabbed her big ass increasing both our pleasures.

We came up for air panting like crazy. I picked Summer up over my shoulders. She squealed as I took her to my bedroom and threw her on the bed. I lay beside her, and she said my strong sexy boy. Summer said I loved you admiring my body. I said I loved doing it, when I saw your thighs today, I became horny as hell.

Summer said I know how much you love my thick white thighs. I smiled at her and massaged her big titties. Summer said I'm glad you have your own place; I can come visit you and we can fuck. I said I look forward to your visits.

Summer said what do you want for dinner. I told her what I wanted for dinner. Summer and I checked the refrigerator. She said we have to go to the supermarket. I said I think we do since I don't have anything the best cook in the world needs to make us dinner. Summer smiled at me lovingly and puts her hands on my face gently.

We put on some clothes and went to the supermarket. We got all the stuff that we needed. Summer was wearing as short skirt that attracted all sorts of attention. The babes at the supermarket were eyeing me and Summer grabbed my hand making sure those bitches know I'm with her.

We went to the cashier, a pretty white girl with the name tag that said Amber. We loaded all the stuff on the belt. Amber said you two make a great couple. I said thanks and so did Summer. Amber said I love interracial sex, my black boyfriend pounds me with his big dick every chance he gets and I love it.

Summer said I love being bent over and fucked by his big black cock. Amber bit her lips and said I'm so wet thinking of you two fucking. Summer said me too and I don't have on any panties. Amber said I love not wearing panties, easy access for stiff chocolate penetration.

Amber scanned the last item and Summer paid her then we started leaving. Amber said it was great meeting you guys. We said likewise walking away from the supermarket. We loaded up my Audi and went back to my apartment.

Summer made us a wonderful dinner. We sat down and ate smiling at each other the whole time. After I was finished eating, I said I miss your wonderful cooking. Summer said I miss you eating like I'm feeding two people. I laughed and said I work out a lot. I need to eat a lot.

Summer said I'm not complaining just saying I miss it. I said ok and she said I love your sexy body with all those muscles and big love muscles. I smiled at her. I left and

Summer did the dishes. She came and cuddled with me on the couch.

Summer said can you take your shirt off while we cuddle, please, we are all alone. I said sure and took my shirt off. Summer ran her hands all over my torso. She said oh my god you're such a work of art. I said thank you Summer.

I said how about a blow job Summer. She said sure baby, lay back let me suck your big cock. I laid back and Summer stroked my bone. She licked my shaft while looking at me with her pretty blue eyes. She engulfed my cock with her warm mouth looking at me in the eyes as she slid her pretty lips up and down my pole.

I moaned oh god so good Summer, you are the best. She stopped and said thank you honey then continued. Summer stopped all of a sudden held my pole then slid her white pussy down it. I squeezed her big tits as she fucked my cock. I moaned oh Summer I love you and she said I love you too my black stud.

Summer creamed my cock a couple of times giving me a vigorous fucking. I put her on her back and pounded her into the couch. Summer moaned oh god honey, you feel amazing in my white pussy. I couldn't take the pressure anymore. I exploded inside of Summer's tight pink hole.

Summer said I love being your cream pie honey. I kissed her and we held each other for a while. I was still inside of Summer when Thad call to check up on her. Summer said the visit is going very well. I made him dinner and we are just hanging out on the couch watching television.

I smiled at Summer as she was lying through her teeth. After they were done talking. Summer said that was naughty taking a call while your dick is still in me. I said oh yeah very naughty smacking her sexy ass.

We kissed then took a naughty shower together. We went to sleep, and I woke up to bacon cooking. I went to the Kitchen and Summer was cooking naked. I hugged her from behind and said good morning naked Summer. She said good morning my sweet chocolate lover boy. We kissed and held each other. Summer felt my hard cock and said do you want to stick it in me, baby. I said oh yeah lifting her up and putting her on the countertop.

I spread her sweet white thighs and penetrated her tight little cunt. I kissed her as she held me tight while I went to town on her pussy. I held her ass and hammered

Summer with all I had. Summer moaned and said oh my god baby, I love getting pounded by you. Summer gave up the cream and a minute later, I ejaculated into her white vagina deeply.

Summer said oh yeah, I love your big cock creaming my pussy. I said I love your tight white pussy so good to me. I said we should eat before it gets cold. We sat and ate smiling at each other like lovers do.

Summer said it's too bad I have to go home today. I'll miss your hard cock always in me. I said I'll miss your tight little cunt always wet and ready for a hard cock. Later, Summer packed up, we hugged and kissed goodbye.

Summer texted me when she got home, and I texted her back missing her and she missed me. The following weekend,

Autumn texted me asking if I wanted to come down to her apartment. I'm on the 20th floor and she is on the 10th floor.

I said sure I went down to her place on Friday night. Autumn was wearing just a t-shirt when I showed up. We sat on the couch and talked, I told her that Summer visited except for the boning a lot part.

We started playing cards on the couch. everything was going great until I saw Autumn's pussy, I became hard as shit. She said oh my god, why are you hard? I said I can see your shaved white pussy between your sweet white thighs. Autumn said oops sorry about that baby. I said its ok you have a very beautiful pussy. She giggled and said you like my thick thighs. I said oh yeah, I've admired your thick thighs for a while.

Autumn said I've seen you looking at my thighs but never thought anything about it. I said now you know, we kept playing cards trying to ignore the sexual tension in the room. Autumn said is that big thing ever going to go down. I said nope.

Autumn said have you ever fantasized about fucking me with that big black pole. I said yeah, she said I've always wanted to see a black cock, can I see yours please.

I said sure Autumn and took my cock out of my pants for her viewing pleasure. Autumn said damn that's huge. I said thanks, she said can I touch it please. I said sure Autumn. She grabbed it quickly and started stroking it before I could possibly say no.

I moaned and Autumn said you like that huh. I said oh yeah don't stop, Autumn took my hand and put it between her sweet white thighs. I rubbed her pussy and she was wet already. I pushed my middle finger into her pussy and wow so good.

Autumn and I were both moaning with the pleasure that we were giving each other. I said this is awesome. I can't believe we are playing with each other like this, Autumn said what's wrong don't you like playing with me. I said I love it, I just can't believe it's happening, it's like a dream come true for me.

Autumn said same here, playing around with a black guy. I said cool then Autumn said do you want to do something cooler. I said sure and she said get on top and stick your black cock in my white pussy.

I said hell yeah, I'd love to do that, Autumn took her t-shirt off and laid back. I said you have a great body and she said you do too stud now stick me with your big black stick. I held her hips and forced my way into her tight pussy. I moaned oh god Autumn I can't believe I'm in you as I started pumping.

Autumn said oh yeah, my first black dick yeah. I squeezed her big tits and fucked her. I moaned oh fuck so good as Autumn creamed my black dick. I said your white pussy is so good Autumn. She replied your black cock is amazing, oh fuck I'm cumming again baby.

I bent her over and smacked her big ass like her hot mama. Autumn said take it baby take it, pull my fucking hair and fill me up like a good little slut. I pulled her hair smacked her ass and said take it you little slut.

I rode the shit out of Autumn as she creamed my cock over and over making me shoot my shot deep in her little white cunt. Autumn fell to the bed and said wow that was amazing thanks for wanting and fucking me. I said my pleasure and the feeling is mutual baby. We kissed each other really hard and grabbed each other's asses.

Autumn said if my mom and dad caught us fucking, they would die. I said they sure would, I'm glad we have our own apartments for privacy. Autumn laughed out loud. We held hands and Autumn said oh crap. I said what's wrong. Autumn said I now see why I was jealous when I saw you with other white girls at school. I said you were secretly hot for me and didn't know it. Autumn said exactly, all the cuddling and hugging didn't help any. I smiled at her lovingly and kissed her sexy lips.

Six months into my sexual relationships with Autumn and summer. My coworker Sarah started hitting on me, being very flirtatious. One day she said what's the matter don't you like white girls or perhaps white pussy.

I said that's not it, I have two fuck buddies who I love. It's my white sister and white mommy. Sarah said oh wow I didn't see that coming. I said see, now you won't be talking to me anymore. Sarah said fuck that I still want you. My mouth popped open and my eyes doubled in size.

Sarah said I'm a kinky white bitch and I want your black cock in me. So, there it is all out on the table. Sarah kissed me and I grabbed her big ass, we went at it for a little while. We heard someone coming and stopped. Sarah said this isn't over, we are going to definitely continue this later baby. I said hell yeah.

A week later, Sarah texted me asking if I was banging my other 2 sluts. I said not at the moment. She said I'm horny and wet lying in my bed naked. I want you to come over and penetrate my white vagina until you ejaculate your hot sperm inside of me.

I said oh wow Sarah, I want you too badly baby. Sarah sent me a naked picture of her in bed with her awesome body. I said send me your address and I'll be right over. I was surprised when she texted me her address. It was the 30th floor of our luxury apartment tower.

I put on some clothes and went up to her apartment. I rang the doorbell. Sarah opened the door totally naked with a smile on her pretty face. Her blonde hair up in a bon wearing those sexy red glasses.

I locked the door, Sarah hugged me and kissed me as we fell against the door. Sarah jumped on my hips and I dropped my pants. She slid down my hard-black pole, impaling her tight little cunt on my penis. Sarah moaned oh yeah, your big black cock is deep in my white cunt, I want to be your slut too baby. I kissed her and put her on the door. I pounded the shit out of Sarah, oh my god so good giving it to her. I've admired her for so long working on the stadium. She is in charge of the lights and electrical systems. The sparks flew as we fucked like animals on the door.

Sarah said oh my god so good as she came on my cock. She said take me to my bedroom. I carried her to her bedroom. I threw her fine ass on the bed. I jumped on her and penetrated her again. I gave her a proper roman fucking until I could take no more and released my pleasure inside of her.

Sarah said that was a long time coming, I've been wanting to take my panties off for you since you joined the company. I said I've noticed your sexy ass jiggling around the office for my viewing pleasure. Sarah said I've seen you checking out my thighs, ass and big tits.

I said I love your body every inch of it, massaging her sweet white thighs, tits and ass. Sarah said oh yeah run your chocolate hands all over my vanilla body. I kissed her as I ran my hands all over her wonderful goodies.

Sarah said stay with me tonight and you can go home in the morning since we have work tomorrow. I said ok baby. We cuddled up naked and slept the night away. I woke up spooning Sarah, she felt my hard cock and said how about some morning cock before you go lover. I said my pleasure holding her hips and penetrating her from behind.

I squeezed her big tits and gave her the morning cock she so desired roughly. Sarah said oh my god baby you're so rough, I love it, give it to me. I gave it to her and Sarah gave my shaft some morning cream for my troubles. I fucked her faster and faster until I filled up her pleasure tank with my love gas.

I kissed Sarah and we held each other tight. I said I better go to my apartment and get ready for work. Sarah said I need to shower so I don't smell like sex at work. I said me too. Sarah jiggled to the shower looking at me. I put on my clothes and left to go to my apartment. Sarah said enjoy your walk of shame after getting some of my white pussy. I laughed out loud and left.

I went to my apartment, showered and got ready for work. I grabbed breakfast on the way to work. I was in my office when Sarah texted me that she was walking around the office with my sperm in her vagina and loving every minute of it.

Sarah walked by my office smiled and winked at me. I texted her that I love my cream pie little slut walking around the office with my sperm in her vagina. Sarah said I love being your little slut for pleasure.

I went back to work then went home for the day later. Weeks later, my doorbell rang and it was Summer coming to see me. She didn't have her suitcase so I guess she wasn't staying. I said come in and she kissed me. Summer said god, I missed you, I just need to see you and feel you.

Summer took her dress off and said your little slut needs you on top of her. Summer took my hand and we went to my bedroom. She laid down and I mounted her plunging my dagger of love inside her deep. Summer held me tight and said take it my black stud.

I pounded the shit out of Summer and she fucking loved every second of it creaming my dick like crazy. I held her shoulders and gave her the finishing touches. I cream pied her sexy ass to my bed. Summer held me and kissed me like crazy. She said stay in me until you go soft my love.

We were in our own little world when Autumn came into my room and said surprise. I jumped off of Summer and Autumn said oh my god mom you like black cock too. Summer said sorry honey please don't tell your father I'm fucking our adopted black son.

Before she could answer, Summer said wait a second why are you naked, are you fucking him too. Autumn said yeah, I'm his little slut too. I became hard again seeing naked Autumn looking at my cock and biting her lips.

She said I can't wait; I came for cock and I'm taking it. She straddled me and slid her white vagina down my hard-black penis. Summer said oh wow hard again so soon. I said oh yeah, I can't get enough white pussy. Autumn and I can't get enough of your black dick. She fucked me like she meant it, I said oh yeah you little slut take that dirty cock with your mothers cream on it.

Autumn said oh yeah fuck your dirty little slut, she screamed and creamed my cock as Summer watched with her mouth open wide and eyes doubled in size. I was so turned on I dumped Autumn on the bed and mounted her properly. I fucked the shit out of her with no mercy as her mommy watched. I filled her with my love juice and she took the pounding like a good little slut.

We kissed then I laid between Summer and Autumn. I held their hands and we took a little nap. We were awoken by Sarah, she said these must be your two other sluts. Autumn the ever feisty one said who is this bitch. I said this is my office slut. Summer said oh I'm his white mommy and Autumn said sorry I'm his white sister. Sarah said it's a pleasure to meet both of you, I've heard so much about you two horny little cunts.

The end

www.ingramcontent.com/pod-product-compliance
Lightning Source LLC
LaVergne TN
LVHW020544160826
845677LV00015B/4187

9798352104439